The Rapier

by

Don Thomas

BOOK.ROBBENT.COM
A ROBB ENTERTAINMENT CORPORATION COMPANY

ROBB
PUBLISHING
online media group

comics.robbent.com

Your digital source for media and entertainment.

Robb Weekly News

Don Thomas is a writer who lives in Tennessee
and has published several books and comics
over the years. He also works as a professional
editor and worked on various prose anthology
magazines. He is represented by Robb Talent
Group (rtg.robbent.com).

ROBB
ENTERTAINMENT
merchandising
merch.robbent.com

CHAPTERS

Chapter One:

The Morning After

Detective Smith's phone had been ringing all morning. Seems a Hollywood starlet was abducted from her home in the middle of the night. He'd crossed paths with her earlier in the week while investigating a robbery attempt at the Los Angeles museum. Considering that case involved a body being hacked to pieces there might be a connection.

Before he could even have his usual morning coffee or read the paper he was dressed and headed out the door. A six year veteran, Detective Smith was used to arriving at crime scenes before the body was cold. However, when he got to the house, he had to admit it wasn't what he expected.

He took a look at the victim. His name was Jonas Murphy. He worked for Ms. Reynolds as a handyman, fixing things and doing whatever chores needed to be done. From the looks of things, Murphy realized someone was breaking into the house and tried to call for help, but the phone lines had been cut. When they busted into the house and found him in the kitchen frantically trying to use the phone, they were on him like a pack of hungry dogs.

It was a grisly scene and he was used razor blade slayings. His thoughts went to the Japanese swords from the attempted heist at the museum. He imagined two or three assailants welding one of those weapons would be able to inflict that sort of damage to an unarmed opponent. It was a very different type of murder than Detective Smith was used to.

"And that's just where the differences begin," he thought as he headed into the living room where the other detectives were interviewing Jason Graves, the man who survived the attack.

Graves was a popular film star and friend of Gloria Reynolds and there were rumors the two of them were romantically involved. Which meant there wasn't anything surprising about him being at her house at such an odd hour of the night. What was unusual was Graves wasn't just your average run of the mill problem-making, pleasure-seeking actor. He was also, according to recent news, the first costumed adventurer, if you believe that sort of thing. A couple of weeks earlier at the premiere of his new movie he managed to distract a couple of real-life heavies long enough for the cops to show up.

Not surprisingly, the Hollywood press had blown things completely out of proportion. Soon, headlines all over the country featured Graves as supposedly some sort of hero. Smith knew most of the guys on the force thought it more of a joke or a studio publicity stunt than anything else.

Graves was a troublemaker, always getting caught with his pants down, sleeping around with any dame that would give him the time of day. He also had a habit of drinking too much and more than once someone on the force had to break up a barroom brawl that Graves started. To put it bluntly, he was a degenerate. He also had a hard time keeping his mouth shut. If he hadn't worked for one of the biggest movie studios in the city, he probably would have been run out-of-town a long time ago.

"One thing I know for damn sure is I'm no help to Gloria wasting my breath talking to you guys.. They took her, I'm going after her and that's the end of it!" Jason Graves said angrily as Detective Smith entered the room.

"Mr. Graves, I assure you the department is doing everything it can to find Ms. Reynolds. This includes gathering as much evidence and information from anyone and everyone who was here when the crime was taking place. Last time I checked, the only witness they left alive was you.".

Jason thought about it for a moment, and Smith's words seemed to settle him down. "It had to be the same group of thugs. Not local guys. Not this time. The guy I fought was wearing some sort of antique Japanese armor," he added.

"Armor huh? Is that why he was able to give you that lump on your head?" Smith's partner asked.

Jason smiled. If I had thought to bring my gun, I would have killed every single one of the sonsofbitches and you guy's would all be sitting at home eating your morning breakfast."

"I'm sure." Smith's partner said dryly.

"Don't worry about him Graves; just tell us exactly what happened." Detective Smith said.

He grabbed a gold case from his inside pocket, pulled out one of his custom rolled cigarettes and lit it. "It was already late by the time you were finishing questioning us after the attempted robbery at the museum. My driver drove straight to Gloria's place. She invited me up for a nightcap. I told Charlie to head on home and come back to pick me up in the morning."

"Good enough a friend to invite you to spend the night in her bed?" Smith asked.

"I've known her since the early days. We worked together on our first studio picture. The very first time I saw her, we were shooting an ice skating scene. She was drop dead sexy and just dripped charisma. Athletic and competitive. She has always been what I wanted. But no, usually she wouldn't give me the time of day as far has any bedroom shenanigans. Don't think I haven't tried. But then those thugs crashed the premiere of my movie and all of a sudden the press is calling me a costumed vigilante. Then the studio buys into the whole masked hero idea and the next thing I know I'm actively trying to play a positive role in the community. Gloria saw that, she read it in the papers. Then at the attempted robber at the museum she saw with her own two eyes that I was willing to risk my life to save other from harm. I am sure the both of you know exactly what I am talking about. It happened and it was everything I had ever hoped it would be. But I don't see how explaining all of this out gets us one inch closer to rescuing the woman I love."

"Maybe she just has a thing for guys who like to wear costumes. I've heard about those Hollywood dames being in to that kinky stuff." Smith's partner suggested.

"Joe, that's enough. This man didn't commit the crime and he certainly isn't a suspect. From what I saw at the premiere, he's honestly trying to help. Why don't you step out and get a couple of cups of coffee for the both of us?" Detective Smith suggested.

"You sure?" Joe asked hesitantly.

"Yeah, I'm sure," Smith sighed. "Mr. Graves, how do you like yours?"

"A little sugar, but hold the cream. Now… where was I?" Graves asked.

"Your friend had invited you up for a nightcap," Detective Smith reminded him.

"Oh yeah; so she invited me up for a nightcap, and one thing led to another, and we ended up in her bedroom for the rest of the night. Like I said, it had been a rough evening. She had fallen asleep I was lying there . Suddenly I heard some noises coming from downstairs. Sounded like someone had broken in. Actually, it sounded like several people had broken in. Then someone downstairs shouted out, trying to warn us."

"Jonas Murphy, the handyman?" the detective suggested.

"Yes, probably, it sounded like Jonas. Poor guy, he deserved better than that," Graves said, his words filled with a tangible bitterness for such an undeserved death.

"Yeah, no one deserves being cut down like that. So what did you do at that point?" Smith prodded.

"Wasn't a lot that I could do, not without weapons and having no time to react. The phone was out too. I heard a scuffle, but I wasn't going to let them do the same thing to me and Gloria without a fight. So I woke her up and told her to hide. Meanwhile I put my pants on and hid behind the door and waited."

"And what happened then?"

"At that point they were searching for Gloria—you know, going from room to room. I'm not sure if they were expecting me there or not, but I tell you one thing, they were well armed and ready for anything."

"Why do you say that?" Detective Smith asked putting together the images of the viciously slashed murder victim in his mind with the information Jason was giving him about the attackers. Whoever and whatever they were connected to, it didn't seem likely that Graves would feel much of a need to embellish his story.

"Unlike the men at the premiere, these guys were fully armored and decked out with multiple Japanese swords. Or at least the guy that busted into her room was," Jason continued.

Smith pressed him. "What did you do when he entered the room?"

Graves' eyes narrowed, remembering. "I did what I could, as soon as he entered I charged up and knocked him hard in the face. Between how hard I punched him and the fact I took him by complete surprise, I managed to knock him to his knees with that first punch."

"Sounds like a pretty good punch."

"Desperation tends to make a man punch harder than usual." Graves added, his voice taking on a hard note.

"So I've been told. What happened next?" Detective Smith kept at him.

"He started to go for his sword so I tackled him and we started rolling back and forth on the carpet. I managed to get on top of him, using my fists and repeatedly punching him in the face and head. Eventually he stopped moving," he admitted.

"Do you think you killed him?" Smith wondered.

"I hope so," Graves said without remorse, "Especially if he had anything to do with killing Jonas. Since they didn't leave his body, hard to say. Next thing I know a couple of them came up behind me, grabbed me and knocked me me senseless."

"Anything else happen before you lost consciousness?" Smith asked.

"Yeah, one of the guys behind me, probably the leader, made a point of telling the others not to kill me. Said he wanted me left alive at least for the moment." Jason said visibly shaken by the whole ordeal.

"Why would he do that?" Smith asked, because it sounded bizarre.

"Something about it wouldn't be a death worthy of a hero. He said he had other plans for me." Graves sounded more angry than concerned.

"That doesn't sound good."

"No, it doesn't," he said flatly. "Are we done here?"

"Yeah, for now," Smith told him. "Just promise me you'll sit tight and not do anything foolish."

"I can't promise you I'm just going to sit back and do nothing, but I guarantee it won't be anything foolish," Graves stated.

"Fair enough," the detective said with a resigned sigh. "I can understand you wanting to help."

Detective Smith escorted the movie star downstairs where Jason Graves gathered the rest of his things and headed outside. His driver, Charlie Gunn, was waiting to take him home. "You okay boss?" Gunn asked.

"No, Charlie. I'm not OK, but there's not much I can do about that here. Let's get going," he told his good friend. "

As they headed back to his estate, Jason Graves found himself reflecting on the series of events that led to where he was tonight, crossing paths with murderous scum and a bad guy right out of the comics. Sometimes life was even stranger than fiction. It all started when he got involved in a new swashbuckling movie called, The Rapier.

Chapter Two:

The

Interview

Jason Graves' driver and right-hand-man, Charlie Gunn, always made sure to get him up right before dawn on days when he had appointments. They both knew how important it was for him to keep this one in particular and to look presentable the entire time. Jason had to take pains to stay under control. He only drank four or five scotches the evening before, instead of the usual amount.

Still, Jason had to give himself twenty extra minutes in the scalding water trying to draw off all vestiges of his perpetual hangover. That was something Jason had become better at, shaking off the effects of his strenuous nocturnal debaucheries. When stardom was thrust upon him, it became necessary to have longer periods of sobriety. He turned the water off and quickly dried himself and then put on a pair of boxers and grabbed the robe that was laid out for him. The shower had helped and he was feeling better by the second.

Over the years Jason managed to build up his endurance and he had not always been so reckless. He was a track and field star back in high school. He even ran in the New York and Boston marathons and was still in pretty good shape. He had always pushed himself in every way. When they shot a movie he was usually one of the very last of the crew to want to call it a day. Jason was proud of his athletic prowess, as it was something he had worked hard to develop.

"But then again, look who I'm comparing myself to," he said to himself as Charlie came into the room with both arms full of clothes. Charlie was not as young as Jason, but had a warrior's build and carried the load with little effort. They knew each other well, so no words were needed between them as Jason quickly went through the wardrobe options for that morning. He decided on a pair of white pants and a brilliant blue button down shirt, with a t-shirt underneath.

The phone rang and Charlie left the room to answer it while Jason got dressed. After a few minutes, Charlie came back and knocked on the door, telling Jason that the reporter from the Los Angeles Times would be there soon. Jason called to him that would be fine and that he was almost ready.

By the time that Jason made it down the stairs and into the kitchen, Charlie was already pouring him a cup of coffee.

"Here you go boss," he said handing it off.

"Thanks Charlie. So…?"

"So…what?" Charlie asked.

Graves took a sip. "The reporter? What did she sound like?" He had that rakish grin.

"Old," was the noncommittal reply.

"Old?" That wasn't promising.

"Yeah, she sounded old."

Now it sounded bizarre. "Why would the send some strange old woman to interview me?"

"She's a reporter, not a date."

"You say tomayto and I say tomahto."

"No, I say this one was old, like your grandmother. You gonna be alright today boss? I know you are between jobs and stuff, and that usually means you party like there's no tomorrow."

Graves waved him off. "Charlie, that was yesterday. Today I'm going for my wardrobe fitting for that new movie."

"It's just that I don't know how that's going to work out for you; some guy prancing around in tights with a sword and he somehow manages not to get shot."

"Gee, when you put it like that, it does sound horrible."

Jason grabbed the coffee pot and poured himself another cup. He'd known Charlie for most of his life, and the two of them somehow survived that prison camp some called Brooklyn. Jason managed to get a scholarship to an acting school in California. The right person caught him performing the Saint Crisins Day speech from Shakespeare's Henry V. The prize money was just enough to finance his move to the West Coast. After, six months of additional acting classes, he started auditioning for roles.

"She'll be here soon. You sure you're up for this?" Charlie asked.

" I'll be fine. You can stop worrying. I promise I won't embarrass you."

"Nah, it's not that. I've just got other things on my mind," Charlie said as he walked over to the counter making a point to avoid eye contact with his friend and employer the entire time.

"Listen, I don't know what you are so concerned about. We both know this is how the game works. The more publicity I get, the more acting roles the studio throws at me. The more acting roles I get, the more things I get to buy. The more income I get my hands on, the more some of it eventually trickles down to you. You know, just like Ronnie was talking about the other day at the club."

"Sounds like a great plan if you're the guy with all the money. That's not the problem. You see, the other day the guys were telling me about this charity event for the orphanages in the city. An amateur boxing event."

"Don't tell me, your friends conned you into fighting some guy. You know, sometimes I just don't understand how those guys get you to do stuff like this. What if you get hurt? Some of those boxing guys are pretty rough, and your last fight was…when? Years ago and how well did that go?"

"I survived. But don't worry, I can promise you I won't be the one getting knocked around this time."

"How can you be so sure?"

"I just am...I...I just don't want to get into it now. I'll explain after the interview."

Jason could tell Charlie was hiding something, but he wasn't sure what. He knew his friend had a knack for getting in way over his head. It was what put him in the situation where he had to drop everything and abandon his life in New York and come to California. To this day, Jason continued to receive letters from Charlie's sister asking him why her brother had just packed up his things and left in the middle of the night.

Jason usually tried to cover for Charlie, convincing her he had just offered his friend more money than he could refuse. He didn't try to hide the fact things were to the point on the West Coast where he was having trouble figuring out who he could trust and who he couldn't and having Charlie nearby was comforting. It wasn't exactly a lie and it wasn't exactly the truth either. There was little doubt Jason had benefited from Charlie coming out to California to work for him, but the fact was things had been getting dangerous in New York for his longtime friend. Charlie had made the wrong kind of enemies, the type that would come looking not only for you, but also your family. So, after a desperate late-night phone call explaining what was going on, the two of them agreed it would be best for Charlie to move.

His friend was in Los Angeles for only about week before he decided it wasn't right for him to just sit there and accept Jason's generosity. Before Jason knew it, Charlie had taken over the responsibilities of several of Jason's hired staff and he was able to let them go. Charlie it seemed just wasn't the type of guy to just sit around and do nothing and Jason could see how much his friend wanted to help pay him back for his generosity, so he went along with it. It was an arrangement that worked for both of them.

Jason drank the last of his coffee and handed Charlie the cup. And as he left the kitchen, his friend followed him down the hallway. Although Charlie had worked for him for several years, Jason was still not used to having someone who was always there for him. He had lived in California and worked as a struggling actor for over a year before he managed to get cast in the lead of his first film, so he was accustomed to dog-eat-dog partnerships.

Eventually the money and everything that comes with it started flowing in and before he knew it Jason let it go to his head. He always found it difficult to turn down a good time and suddenly it seemed liked everyone was his friend. The problem was, everyone didn't have his best interests in mind. There were a lot of sharks in Hollywood and plenty of other guys waiting in the wings to take his place. When he found out his old friend Charlie was in a rough spot he was more than a little relieved his best friend would be leaving the city of New York behind and joining him in Los Angeles. When they were growing up, Charlie was always the voice of reason and probably the best friend and protector a man like Jason could ever hope for.

Charlie had watched out for him growing up and it felt good to return the favor. The two of them made it to the spacious living room when they heard the horn from the car outside.

"That's probably her. You stay here and I'll check it out," Charlie said as he opened the door and headed outside. He walked quickly down the driveway. Jason watched his friend the entire time as he made his way towards the front gate. Being in California agreed with Charlie, much like it had agreed with him.. Jason figured that sometimes Charlie missed New York City, but it was hard to tell because his friend just wasn't the type to complain. Sometimes Jason wondered what he would have done if Charlie hadn't agreed to come to work for him.

"Probably would've just placed an ad in the paper or something and I bet I could have gotten a tall red-head with long legs instead," Jason mused to himself as his friend opened the gate and let the reporter's car in. She pulled the car up the driveway and parked it in front of the house. To Jason's surprise it was a younger woman, in a conservative outfit with her hair up. As she got out of her car Jason opened the door and started walking towards her.

"I see you've already met Charlie. I'm Jason Graves."

"I know who you are Mr. Graves. I doubt there are many people in America that wouldn't immediately recognize you."

"Thanks, that's pretty flattering. You know, not everyone has seen my films. The other day we were in Bakersfield and the man pumping gas didn't recognize me. In fact, he said he had no idea who I was and he had never seen a single one of my movies."

"Then how did he know you had been in films before?" she asked pointedly.

"Because I told him…" he said with a smirk.

"I would imagine that would be an easy thing for a man who has appeared in over a dozen movies in the last six years to get accustomed to. I'm Laura Langely, by the way." Miss Langely said as they shook hands. Afterward Jason held onto her hand and slowly kissed the back of it, his concentrated gaze speaking volumes before letting go.

"Uhmm…" she pulled her hand back reluctantly. "My editors warned me about you."

"Did they?" he said with a half-smile, turning on the charm.

"Yes, indeed they did." She smiled back.

"Good. I always appreciate a challenge. I think we would both probably be more comfortable if we conducted the interview inside though, too many gawking tourists out here. Charlie, why don't you make yourself useful and fix us something to drink?"

Charlie glanced over at Jason uneasily. So did the woman. They both knew Jason Graves' reputation with alcohol.

"Charlie makes some of the best iced tea this side of the Rocky Mountains," he added, and everyone relaxed.

Miss Langley smiled, "That would be fine; it's starting to look like another hot summer day and a glass of tea sounds great."

Jason's friend breathed a sigh of relief and then headed into the house ahead of them, to fix their drinks. Jason was being his usual unpredictable self, but Charlie was still hopeful he would get through the interview without any problems.

When Jason was doing the Hollywood thing, hobnobbing with the celebrities, entertainment reporters and the like, Charlie usually liked to keep his distance. This was the world Jason had been born for and Charlie understood it required charisma, charm, and just a bit of an ego. He was Jason's friend and always willing to lend a hand, but figured the best thing he could to to help was to keep his mouth shut and concentrating on cleaning up the messes his friend sometimes made of his life.

Jason and Laura talked for a couple of hours and most of that time she was busily writing down notes for the article she would later write. For most of the conversation Charlie stayed slightly out of earshot, but he did notice when he went to refresh their drinks Jason was telling her about how much he was influenced by the early work of Douglas Fairbanks.

Jason had taken Doug's recent death pretty hard and he went on a lengthy drunken binge that started out as something of a personal wake for his good friend. It quickly degenerated into the type of excess and hedonism which would probably have shocked the most open-minded liberal. Eventually, Charlie was able to get his friend to slow down before it was too late. Luckily, all it ended up costing them was one lone tooth in the back of Charlie's mouth. The fight they had seemed a sort of turning point for Jason, though it was too early to tell.

The next time Charlie entered the room to see how they were doing, Jason asked him to bring up the car because Miss Langley wanted to go with him for his costume fitting for the new movie. She said she wanted to have some publicity photos of Jason taken in full costume for the article. Charlie left to get the car. Mrs. Langley made a quick call to her paper to let them know that she needed a photographer to meet them at the studio.

By the time Charlie brought the car to the front of the house they were already outside and Jason was giving her a quick tour of the carefully landscaped front of the estate. Charlie pulled the car up, got out and opened the door and soon they were on their way to the studio. There wasn't a lot of conversation, although Charlie did notice that Miss Langely was sitting close to Jason and he caught his friend putting his hand on her leg as he whispered something in her ear. Charlie wasn't sure what Jason said to her, but she seemed to appreciate it. She smiled and inched just a bit closer, placing her hand on top of his..

The studio already had Jason's measurements and all the costumes and wardrobe for his new action adventure project had already been created, so this was more to decide if any slight changes needed to be made. The first outfit Jason showed them was for the ballroom scene and was something like what his aristocratic character might have worn at the beginning of the film, before dire circumstances would force him to become the roguish swashbuckling hero.

Miss Langely seemed genuinely impressed and told him he wore that type of clothing well. Jason smiled and as the seamstress double-checked the fitting, he told the reporter sometimes he felt more comfortable wearing the period outfits than modern-day clothing. After the seamstress completed her job the photographer took a few quick shots of Jason.

There were only a couple more fittings after that one and Jason had purposely saved the "Heroic" costume for last. He made sure to not only came out in the costume, but with all the props as well.

"You look absolutely dashing," she gushed.

"Thanks, it's a bit tight in some places, but certainly not the worst thing I've ever had to wear for a movie. You like?"

"Oh yeah, I like."

"Good. Very good", he said trying not to gloat.

"Why don't you tell me about this particular film role while Sam snaps a couple of photos."

His work was something Jason enjoyed talking about. "In this film, the man I'm portraying has been a sort of dandy, living an easy life considering the harsh times he was born in. He's gotten into a lot of trouble because of gambling debts and his parents have sent him to live with his uncle who was the colonial governor of one of the smaller islands in the Caribbean. However, when he gets there, he discovers his uncle was killed and replaced by Lord Craddick, who is more interested in exploiting the locals for his own personal gain. So he decides to don this costume to disguise his self to rally the people to overthrow Craddick. Which he feels will avenge the death of his uncle."

"Sounds pretty heroic."

"I guess, but then again it is an adventure movie set in a historical period. Of course in modern life, if a guy dressed up in a silly costume and walked around in broad daylight, he'd quickly find himself on a one way trip to the nuthouse."

"You're probably right about that, but then again this is the twentieth century."

Jason sighed. He hated to let those roles go, they were a lot of fun. "Well it looks like I'm about finished here and you probably have enough to write your article. How about the two of us go grab something to eat for a late lunch? I know this great little place I think you would love and it would give us a chance to get to know each other better."

Miss Langely smiled, slightly blushed and then told him she would be delighted.

"Great, just give me a chance to change and we'll be on our way."

Jason quickly changed back into his regular clothes and they headed to the car. They stepped outside the building and one of Jason's co-stars met them outside the door. He was the older actor who was playing the uncle who gets killed early on in the picture.

"Hey Jason, it's good to see you."

"Same here Nate, are you here to be fitted for your wardrobe too?"

"Yeah, although since I'm only in a few short scenes there's not a whole lot for me to be fitted for. But I'm glad I ran into you. I wanted to wish you luck. That's a hell of a generous thing you're doing tonight. Most guys would have just written a check and been done with it. But not you, you're actually willing to jump into the ring with another guy and take a couple of shots to the face if it can raise money to help a good cause like those poor orphans."

"Huh?" Jason Graves said having no idea what he was talking about.

"Don't be so modest Jason, it's really a great thing you're doing here, I bet you didn't even mention it during your interview."

"Yeah, thanks, I guess," he said still a little confused.

It must be something he agreed to do when he was drunk. He boxed a little at the club, but not often.

Miss Langely put her arm around him and gave him a quick kiss on the cheek. "I have to say, I'm also impressed."

"Thanks doll. Sorry I didn't tell you about it earlier. Anyway Nate, always good to see you and I hope you'll be able to catch my little exhibition fight for charity. I could certainly use the support in my corner."

"I wish I could, but I promised the wife I'd take her out for her birthday tonight and she's never been much of a fan of boxing. She says that the idea of two men slugging at each other is a little too barbaric for her tastes."

Something didn't sound right. "Wait… did you say her birthday was today?"

"Yeah, so sorry about not being able to watch you fight."

"Tonight?" Jason was truly surprised by this.

Nate was unsure what Jason was asking "I'm sorry, what?"

"You can't watch me fight tonight, because you have previous plans with your wife." Jason sounded slightly incredulous.

"That's right Jason. Is… something wrong?"

"Nah, not really," he lied, "It must have slipped my mind. That's right, I'm fighting tonight." Now Jason started to recall that Charlie had said this morning he had something going on with boxing. Things began to make sense.

"Happens to the best of us, just more so when you get older. I guess I'll see you again when we start shooting."

"Nate, be sure to give the wife a birthday kiss for me."

"Yeah, she'll love getting that," Nate said and was gone.

Jason and Laura continued on to the car, where Charlie was waiting for them. As Charlie opened the door for Laura , Jason gave him a look.

"What's up boss?" Charlie asked him.

Jason frowned. "Let's just say I figured out why you were so confident earlier about not getting hurt doing that little 'favor' for your friend."

"Oh, that." He sounded guilty.

"Yes, that. when were you planning on letting me know about it, Charlie?" Jason asked as he stepped into the vehicle.

"Is something wrong?" Laura asked as Charlie got inside the car and started up the engine.

"Too soon to tell. Just looking out for a friend," Jason added.

"Right boss, always looking out for others, that's you," Charlie said as he adjusted his cap.

Jason knew at that point if he tried to back out of the fight he would end up looking like a jerk, and even worse like a spineless coward, which he certainly wasn't. He decided to go easy on the lunch and skipped the usual three or four drinks, since he was fighting in a couple of hours. He also decided it would probably be best if he took Miss Langely to a restaurant instead of his bedroom and he had originally planned. And that was how Jason Graves ended up at the close of the day to facing off in the ring against a professional boxer.

He still couldn't believe how the events of the day had turned. There he was, sitting in one corner of the boxing ring, looking across to the other side. His opponent was a man who was so at home in the ring, he looked like he had escaped his mother's womb complete with trunks and wearing his own pair of boxing gloves. This guy was a professional boxer; his arms were thick with the kind of muscles known for teaching other men the error of getting into the ring with them.

It was a warm California night and already beads of sweat had started descending down Jason's naked chest. Although the daredevil in him wasn't afraid of the beating he was probably about to receive, he did hope the guy he was matched up against would think he was. It might give him a slight advantage and Jason knew he would have to make serious use of any possible advantage. Charlie told him the man he was fighting in this exhibition bout had been fairly successful as an amateur boxer in the Marine Corps and from there professionally up and down the West Coast for the last couple of years. He was good enough to have earned a record of eighteen fights that included eleven TKO's.

The announcer climbed into the ring and walked over to Jason's corner to greet him. "Mr. Graves, it's good to see you so ready and willing to do your part for the orphans of Los Angeles. When I first heard you had signed up for this, I thought they were making some sort of mistake. But it's nice to see there's more to you than what appears in the scandal pages."

Jason shrugged. "I'll take that as a compliment. But if you don't mind I would rather you sped things up a bit. Whichever one of us that ends up on the mat, he needs to do it soon, because I've already made plans for the rest of the evening." Jason said as he turned and looked over to the young brunette reporter who had decided to let her hair down to watch the fight.

She wore a slightly uncomfortable smile, which quickly changed into something more enthusiastic as Jason and the announcer looked over in her direction. She had also changed the shade of lipstick she was wearing to a much deeper red, which did much to contrast with the way she had looked earlier that day. She had agreed to come, but said she feared being recognized, especially since this was less like reporting and more like a date.

"I'll try to keep that in mind," the announcer said with a sly smile as he shook Charlie's hand and then began to walk towards the opposing corner of the ring. After a few quick words to Manny Dugan, Jason's opponent, the announcer stood in the center of the ring and started building up the excitement and interest of the crowd to a fever pitch. At first he pointed over to Manny and let the crowd know about all the boxing accomplishments of the big, burly man who Jason was about to fight.

Jason knew it would not be long before the announcer would turn to him. There wouldn't be much to tell, at least not as far as boxing went. Jason had fought a couple of easy bouts here and there. Maybe something to brag about late at night in a darkened bar than anything else. But the simple truth was, once his career had taken off as a movie actor, he quickly decided to give boxing up. Honestly, after his chauffeur Charlie gave up what little boxing career he had enjoyed on the East Coast, Jason didn't see any reason to continue pursuing such a potentially dangerous sport. Actors depended too much on their looks.

Yet there he was, about to fight a guy with at least twenty pounds of muscle over him, all because someone had convinced Charlie it was something I might be interested in. But he did like the orphanage angle. That sort of press was almost worth getting punched in the face. Problem was, Charlie was never one for the details.   down. He didn't want to lose the fans that thought more of him then he really deserved, and he didn't want to disappoint his loyal friend.

"You ready, boss?" Charlie said, playing the role of his ring manager.

 "As ready as I can get. Just thinking Maybe I could just go a few rounds with someone else a bit softer and curvier tonight," Jason, said giving a quick look and wink at the reporter before standing up to hear the referee explain the rules.

The other guy wasn't much for talking, but Jason made sure to ham it up a bit for the crowd. He had always been a bit of a showman and wasn't about to let such an opportunity pass. He waved to the crowd and acted every bit as surprised he was going to face off against such a dangerous looking opponent.

They went back to their corners and when the bell rang, the two men came out and exchanged a couple of punches. Jason did his best to keep his distance, trying to gauge what type of boxer his opponent was. That didn't take long because this guy was pressing the attack, quickly coming at Jason with a flurry of blows, even managing to deal a couple of solid hits with a wicked right.

For most of the first round Jason did his best to stay on the defensive, concentrating on protecting himself and constantly moving around the ring, trying to use his superior speed. It was a good thing this was just an exhibition match for charity, because it meant it was only going to go five rounds instead of the standard fifteen. By the end of the first round his opponent was starting to get annoyed about having to chase Jason around. The big man started trying to push Graves closer to the ropes so he had nowhere to go and nothing to do but try to block the oncoming punches.

Thankfully Jason was able to avoid getting trapped in one of the corners up until the bell rang. He quickly sat down on the stool Charlie provided and took a quick swig of water, spitting it right back out.

"How are you doing?" Charlie asked.

"Fair enough, but I think he wants to put a pretty bad hurt on me."

"Just keep doing what you are doing. This guy is used to slugging it out, so keep moving and work on that stamina of his. Try throwing a couple of punches to his midsection."

"I'll try," he said as the bell rang and the second round started. This time the other boxer changed up his strategy and kept closing, trying to get in far enough to force Jason to start trading punches. Fortunately, that left him open as he approached. Jason took advantage and hit him a couple of times with a series of quick combinations. It was only at the end of the last series of combos his opponent managed to catch him with that right again.

Jason staggered a step and the other guy pressed the attack with a left that would have probably ended the fight right there, if Jason hadn't managed to somewhat deflect it with his glove. And that was when Manny got what he had wanted from the beginning. Both of them exchanged a flurry of back and forth punches. Jason found himself forced to grab a hold of Manny's arms a couple of times, before things became too heated. The two of them had managed to make their way back to the center of the ring and traded a couple more punches before the bell rang again.

"What happened to concentrating on his gut?" Charlie asked.

"Sorry, I got a bit distracted with him trying to kill me," Jason answered sarcastically.

"He's not trying to kill you. He's just trying to punch your lights out."

"Trying?" Jason said as Charlie wiped the sweat off of his brow and face. He was surprised he'd lasted this long.

The third round was much more Manny's round and he did his best to get Jason to kiss the mat more than once. Once again Jason found himself suffering from that wicked right of his opponent and just doing his best to get in what shots he could. The two of them danced around the ring and threw various punches at each other. In the end, Jason's main accomplishment during the round, was managing to concentrate on Manny's midsection, although it didn't really seem to be that effective a strategy. By the time the bell rang again, Manny was visibly upset an actor had managed to somewhat hold his own against him. Jason went back to his corner where Charlie was waiting for him.

"Listen boss, I saw something out there. Each time he goes to hit you with that power right, he's leaning back just a bit. You've got to pay attention and the next time he does that, take advantage of it. Use it to hit him hard and fast while he's off balance. We both know you aren't going to win this one on points."

"Win this?" Graves almost laughed. "I thought the point was not to get killed."

"I'm telling you, you can win this, but you've got to listen to what I just said and go in there and get it done."

"Yeah, if he doesn't lay me out." At least if he landed some solid blows first, he could go down with dignity in front of Laura Langely.

The bell rang and Jason went out to face his opponent once again. This round Manny decided to end it as soon as he could. He rushed Jason. Manny punched him hard in the face several times. He followed that up with a couple of well-timed combinations. Jason staggered back from the assault and Manny pressed his advantage. He continued to land more punches than Jason could. He even switched up things and managed to score a good solid hit to Jason's gut.

Then Manny caught Jason with yet another solid right. This one was pretty damned effective and it caused Jason to nearly drop right then and there. The punch had done enough of a number on him Manny was able to score a quick combination before Jason managed to get his gloves up enough to somewhat block the attack. He was coming back with the right and then…

There it was, just like Charlie said.

Manny started to lean back, preparing to land another one of his devastating rights. But this time Jason was ready and he struck out with a wicked right of his own that took his opponent completely by surprise. Jason's unexpected punch to Manny managed knocked the other man even more off kilter. Before he could recover, an equally devastating left thrown by Jason knocked Manny completely off his feet and the backside of his body fell flat against the mat.

Jason immediately went to a corner and the referee started counting. Before Manny managed to get back up the count was all the way to seven. The ref looked Manny over, decided he was still fit and continued the fight.

Although those two punches combined with hitting the mat had taken some of the fight out of Manny, he tried to overpower Jason one last time before the bell rang. However, Jason wasn't having any of it and the last thing Manny needed to do was try to press an advantage he really didn't have. It wasn't long before the big man was once again trying to get in a position to put Jason down for the count with another solid right.

Jason was even more ready for this one than the last one. Before Manny knew it, Jason was on top of him, hitting him with one solid right and left after another, not giving him a chance to do anything but be pummeled hard in the face. To Jason's amazement, for the second time that bout, his opponent hit the mat, but this time he wasn't able to get back up before they counted him out.

Laura Langely cheered the loudest, or so it seemed. All Jason Graves could think about is how he wished his friend Doug had been there to see him. He would have loved that fight. Doug would have been proud of him. Hell, Jason was proud of himself, and for the first time since Doug's untimely passing, he didn't celebrate by getting completely drunk.

Chapter Three: Ashes to Ashes

A couple days later, Jason had Charlie pick up Mary around eleven in the morning. He made a promise he would go with her to the cemetery. Even when she had pointed out she had a driver who was more than enough for the task, Jason vehemently objected and told her that Doug wouldn't have wanted her to go alone.

He had been a friend to both of them for almost six years, before and after their marriage. Mary knew Jason had been a big fan of Doug's even before he ever thought about coming to Hollywood and trying to make a name for himself. She understood the friendship Jason had cultivated with his acting idol had been one of his proudest achievements since coming to California.

"Jason, I really don't know why you're making such a fuss. This isn't even a public event, just an old-time entertainer's body being moved to his rightful place of honor," she said as a gloved hand gently touched Jason's own.

"I had to come, Mary, out of respect. The cemetery for legends is far more fitting than where his last wife originally had him buried. If there was ever a man who deserved such, it was Doug. He was my biggest hero...Do you know one time he talked me into jumping off the third floor of the Carlton? Right off one of those little balconies they have, and there was barely enough room for me to get up to full speed. I was damned lucky I didn't crack my head open on the concrete below. I ended up in the pool but only by the slimmest of margins," Jason recounted to her.

"Jason, why did you do something so foolish? You could have been seriously hurt! I always knew Doug had a knack for talking you younger guys into some pretty dangerous stunts, but you should have known better. What if he had told you to go jump from a bridge somewhere, would you have done that too?" she asked.

Jason gave Mary a wry grin and answered, "Only if he was at the bottom goading me on after he had already jumped."

Mary quickly slapped the back of Jason's hands. "You are such a rogue, just like Doug, but you at least should know better. Men with a habit of doing brave things have a way of only living half as long as cowards…"

There was a certain sting to Mary's words, and Jason was obviously troubled by them. He pulled away from her, interlocking both of his arms across his broad chest, and got a serious look on his face. "Doug and I became friends because we understood each other. We both believed it would be a better life to know you might die while being foolishly brave, than just live safely on as just another damned coward. We all know there are plenty of guys in this town who think they're big shots, but in reality are more of the later than the former."

"Spoken like a true acolyte of the church of Doug," she responded and then turned and looked at the window as Charlie continued down the road.

"Mary, I'm sorry, and I certainly didn't mean to upset you. Doug was the type of man they don't make anymore. He was the kind of man I always wanted to emulate. He certainly wasn't perfect, but then again, who is? Not me... I know his death was a bit of a surprise for all of us, but I just don't think he would have wanted any of us to take it as a sign that we should slow down and live each day in absolute fear of death," Jason added.

Mary looked back at Jason and did her best to smile, even as her eyes started to water. "No, he wouldn't have, it's just that I miss the old boy. He was more than just my lover and my husband, he was my friend and a one of the best business partner's one could ever hope to work with. A lot of things about you remind me of him."

"Mary, there's no need to flatter me like that. I fell in love with you a long time ago," Jason said with a warm smile.

She sat there for a second, the blood rushing into her face, bringing a deep red color to both of her cheeks. Just for a moment she reached out and gingerly touched his face. Three fingers gently caressing his cheek. "You are a bit like him. He was always saying things that made my heart flutter. And we both know the press would have a field day at the very thought…"

Jason interrupted her.

"The press doesn't have to know anything. The least I could do for you and for Doug is being here for you."

Mary suddenly withdrew her hand. "You are here for me now Jason. You're also here for Doug and for that, I thank you."

"Don't you want to know?" Jason asked.

"Know what?" Mary replied.

"Wouldn't you like to know the moment, the exact moment I fell in love with you?" Jason queried.

"Jason, I don't think…" Mary started.

"…It was the first time I saw you, there on the silver screen, with those long sausage curls of yours and that great big smile."

That was when Jason got the biggest smile out of Mary that he would get for the entire day. Soon after, the two of them boarded a large yacht that Mary owned, although she seldom used it. But today was a special occasion, and it was carrying special cargo. Mary had arranged Doug a burial site far more fitting than the one in which he was originally buried

When they got to the island, it wasn't long before they were at the tomb Mary had purchased. Although there were only a few witnesses to the reburial, Mary was glad Jason was there, for the truth of it was she hadn't felt so tired and weak in all her life and it felt good to have Jason at her side.

Doug's tomb was in the center of attention in a cemetery that had more than its fair share of centers of attention. At least that was what the cemetery's representative said several times during the dedication. Jason knew the main thing was that Mary had done what she had felt compelled to do. Even if Doug was eventually forgotten, he would have the resting place he deserved.

With the dedication at an end and Doug's remains in their proper resting place, Mary and Jason made their way back to her yacht, and headed back to the mainland. When they disembarked, they found themselves caught in the bright flash of a camera.

"Here Mr. Graves, let me get another picture, but this time pull her closer to you. Maybe even give her a kiss. I can see the headlines now, 'Jason Graves woos dead actor's ex-wife at graveside.' The reporter rattled off even as he quickly changed the burnt out flash bulb.

"Excuse me a second Mary," Jason said as he let go of Mary's arm and started pushing up his sleeves.

When he got into his car, the first thing that Charlie asked him was if he wanted to wait for his friend Mary. "No, Charlie. Mary thought it would be best if she had one of her people drive her back. By the way, catch," Jason added as he tossed a broken camera onto the seat besides Charlie.

"What's this? Somebody taking pictures that they shouldn't?" Charlie asked.

"Nothing to worry about Charlie, I took care of it." Jason explained.

"Damned vultures, I should have gone with you so I could have given the guy a piece of my mind," Charlie said vehemently.

"He could have probably used the extra bit of redirection, but I had the situation well in hand," Jason reassured.

"Alright boss, just making sure. Where you want to go now?" Charlie asked.

Graves frowned. "I wanted to take Mary out for a good meal and a couple of drinks, but since she declined, I see no reason I shouldn't go to the Derby. Get a decent steak and a couple of beers to wash it down with," Jason said.

"And maybe run into Gloria?" Charlie asked.

"Maybe, if I run into her, that is. Not like I'm planning on running into her or anything. If she's there, I might stop by her table and see how she's doing."

"Alright boss, but you know you're scheduled for an early appearance at the the studio in the morning. You gotta start filming that new flick of yours." Charlie pointed out.

There was a sigh. "Oh yeah, you're right. What's the name of this one again?" Jason asked.

Charlie scratched his head. "Darned if I recall. It's the one where you play that pirate that runs around in the tights and a mask. You know sort of like Zorro, but on the water."

"Sounds like a pretty original idea." Jason said sarcastically.

"Yeah right, but we both know you love any opportunity to show off. And from what I heard that's what this gig is all about." Charlie stated.

"Fine, Charlie. Thanks for reminding me. I'll be sure to order a small steak and only a couple of beers, and before you know it, I'll be back to the house and in bed—alone—so that I can get up bright and early. Is that okay with you, mother?" Jason asked with mock sincerity.

"Just letting you know. You're a grown man. You can do what you want." Charlie replied.

"I know Charlie and thanks—seriously."

"You're welcome," his friend said as he steered around a corner, heading toward the restaurant.

It didn't take long before the Maître d' was showing Jason to his usual table. Jason sat down and immediately scanned the room, looking for anyone he recognized, or more importantly, anyone who would recognize him. It looked like the usual crowd, mainly those who worked in the entertainment industry. There were a couple of diners that were obviously a bit star-struck, but so far they hadn't decided to concentrate their full attention on him. That made Jason hopeful the rest of the night would be relatively uneventful and just possibly, his dinner wouldn't be interrupted.

Then he saw her. She must have just arrived or was perhaps in another part of the restaurant. Wherever she had been earlier, there could be little doubt that Gloria Reynolds was making her entrance. It wasn't just that Gloria was stunningly beautiful—a leggy blonde with a figure that most women would kill for—but she also had a way of carrying herself with a confidence and determination that helped make her attractive to everyone, including Jason.

She stopped at a table and bent over to hug one of her female friends, making small talk with several of the customers along the way. That was the thing about Gloria; she didn't care if you were an average Joe off the street or the richest, most powerful man in the room. She treated everyone relatively the same way. Well, maybe not everyone…

"If it isn't Jason Graves. Wasn't expecting to see you out and about. And relatively sober too, with it already being…"

"…Dark out? Thanks doll, but not a drop of liquor has touched these lips all day," Jason stated.

"Uh huh," Gloria replied as she bent down near him, coming close enough he could feel the warmth of her body, even smell the faint fragrance of her perfume. For a moment he thought she was going to kiss him and it was pretty obvious he wouldn't have minded. Then suddenly she snatched up his bottle of beer and took a quick drink.

"That's funny," she said, "I could swear there was alcohol in this half-empty bottle."

"Scout's honor, that's my first drink of the night."

"Honey, if they let you into the boy scouts, then they've recently lowered their standards," Gloria said with dry humor.

"They probably let me in for my tent pitching skills alone," Jason countered smoothly.

Gloria rolled her eyes just a bit at his last words and pulled back away from him. "Same old Jason, pitching tents all over Hollywood. I've heard if you do something long enough you get pretty good at it."

"You have no idea how good or long," Jason quipped right back.

"That's the thing sweet cheeks, not only do I have no idea, I have no interest in ever finding out," Gloria stated flatly. She left him and continued on to her usual spot that was only a few tables away from Jason's own. She sat down facing in his direction and quickly picked up a menu and pointedly used it to block his view of her. After a few minutes they brought out his food and Jason ate as slowly as he could, though Gloria never acknowledged he was there again.

Chapter Four:

The Duel

Charlie made sure he was up and at the studio a few minutes before five. As soon as he arrived, the director let him know they would be filming one of the first fight scenes. It was the one that took place soon after they murdered his uncle and the character he was playing publicly challenges one of the killers at a large social event. It was a fairly crowded opening shot with a roomful of extras and the director thought it would be best if they went ahead and got it out of the way. More importantly, it was the scene where Jason would be wearing the mask and outfit of the signature alter-ego of the movie, another one of the heroic adventurers he was known for portraying. After he put the costume on and had his hair and makeup done, he went over to the prop guy, who had laid out several weapons on a long table for Jason and his opponent to choose from. The guy he would be shooting the fight sequence with was Richard Kensely. Jason had known Richard for several years, and it was not the first time that they had been cast against each other as mortal enemies.

Richard was a good guy and although they traveled in the same circles they were quite different. Jason knew a few years back, Richard had gone through a rather messy divorce and as in his own case, there were always tons of allegations and rumors surrounding Richard and his life outside the movies. But he did wonder if his fellow actor was getting tired of always playing second fiddle to him.

"I had these two made to your exact specifications Jason," the prop master explained as he picked up one of the swords and handed it over. Jason grabbed the weapon to feel the weight of it. He extended it out as far as he could and did a quick couple of slashing motions.

"Great job Murph. This is a quality piece of workmanship. A man could do some serious damage with a weapon like this if he put his mind to it," Jason added.

"Well, don't get any bright ideas. Try to keep in mind we're just shooting a scene. Last time you nearly cut the tip of my finger off," Richard said as he walked up and snatched the other sword.

"Not completely my fault if I remember correctly. No matter how the scene's written, it always seems like you're doing your level best to show everyone you're the better swordsman," Jason replied.

Richard also made sure to check the weight and feel of his own weapon as well. "Two time fencing champion at Princeton, something I shouldn't have to remind you. Then again I can't help they didn't have fencing at the school you went to. I have to say for an amateur, you're really not that bad," Richard admitted.

"Amateur? I may not have went to an Ivy League school but I've worked hard on my swordplay to get it up to speed with guys like you. I certainly know my fair share about handling myself in a fight. Something you should keep in mind, otherwise you might lose something more important than the tip of your finger," Jason firmly stated.

"Bravo! Yes, that's the Jason we all know and love, the shameless braggart. Don't kid yourself, the only reason you end up winning the fight in this scene is because it's been written that way." Richard retorted, even as he chuckled to himself.

Murph the prop master suddenly noticed Jason balling up his left hand into a tight fist and quickly figured out what was about to happen. Before it could go any farther, he stepped in between the two of them, keeping Jason a safe distance from Richard. "Hold on now, I think you two need to stop and you know... save it for the camera. Both of you are acting like you're tykes facing off on the playground."

"He started it," Jason said hotly, playing into it.

"Did not," Richard denied, just as much serious as he was acting.

"Did too!" Jason countered.

"Sheesh! You two are a real riot act. Just try to remember those things are props and have had their blades dulled to lessen the chances of someone getting hurt." The two of them separated and he headed off to towards the director.

"Murph is right Richard, we're not school kids. We are both grown men, with respectable careers," Jason stated.

"You're right Jason, we are both better than that," Richard agreed.

"Thousand dollars to the man who can get the other one to yield first?" Jason suggested roguishly.

"You're on!" Richard agreed and the two of them shook hands to seal the deal.

The stage was set, the extras were brought on wearing their costumes that relatively matched the period the movie called for. The lighting checked, direction was given to the famous and non-famous alike, and, "ACTION!"called. The cameras started to roll. The first opening to this series of scenes didn't include Jason, and was more of a means of showing that the upper crust doesn't have a clue about the current governorship's highly corrupt policies.

By this time in the movie, the character Jason was playing has already seen the death of his uncle by their villainous hands. Because of this, his character decided to side with a small group of pirates who were plaguing the local waters, all of them the sworn enemies of the corrupt authorities. In an effort to protect his friends and family from further attacks by the government, his character elected to put on a mask and create the alter-ego.

Soon the director called, "CUT!", and asked for Jason to come out. It was time to start the scene where he would face Richard's character and the sword fighting sequence would take place. As Jason stepped out on the set, it was obvious the crowd was impressed by his dramatic entrance. His masked buccaneer get-up contrasted greatly with the elegant clothing of the upper class. Once again they made everything ready for the next scene.

"ACTION!" was called, and they began to assume their roles.

"Captain! I would have to disagree with you about the honesty and character of the new governor. He is a tyrant and a wolf-in-sheep's-clothing. Not as yet recognized by the crown and he's only in power because he and his cronies seized the reins of control by assassinating the previous governor." Jason said his lines dramatically, even as he closed the distance between him and his fellow actor, Richard.

"I don't know who you are, but from your foul contempt for authority and your roguish attire, I would assume you're one of those villainous pirates. And if you didn't know, recklessly insulting the new governor is a crime that's punishable by death." Richard stated his lines evenly, even as he drew his own sword.

"A crime punishable by death you say? That seems a bit harsh of a penalty for insulting a man, wouldn't you agree?" Jason said to a woman who stood nearby, who started to smile and nod just a bit as she was directed to.

"You will find I am not a man to be trifled with. I would suggest you throw down your blade and surrender, Before, I decide to wipe that smug smile right off your face," Richard countered, as he closed the distance between them.

…And then with a quickness that took nearly everyone by surprise, Jason pulled out his own rapier and launched a quick thrust towards his fellow actor's throat, a thrust that Richard barely managed to avoid and counter with his own weapon. Suddenly it wasn't just an act.

"Something wrong captain? Something suddenly make you think perhaps I won't be as easy to slaughter as an innocent elderly governor?" Jason asked in character as though he fought in earnest.

"I think you are a braggart and a liar and you and your pirate cohorts are far more responsible for the death of the last governor than anyone else in this room. And one unexpected move seldom makes a man a worthy opponent," Richard quickly replied, the tension mounting between the two.

"Oh it doesn't? Then how about this?"

Then it began; the clashing of swords, the hail of slashing, thrusting, and parrying. The two of them engaged in a deadly dance. The crowd of extras and costars giving them as wide a berth as they could, and making sure not to get in the way of the cameras that were rolling. Both of them made certain to keep at the very edge of the opponent's effective range and with each minor feint, the other responded with several counters.

Back and forth they went, and at first it seemed that Jason Graves's 'Rapier' character had the advantage. Richard's character was not expecting such a skilled opponent, and it was obvious he'd had to gradually up his game and compensate for his opponent's obvious high degree of swordsmanship.

"You are good, that much I have to admit. Much better than the average thieving buccaneer." Richard quoted exactly the line he had memorized earlier but his opinion was sincere. Jason Graves had greatly improved his fencing skills since their last movie.

"The flattery is much appreciated, but I think it would probably be best if you concentrated on the matter at hand. I wouldn't want to embarrass you in front of all of your friends," Jason quipped in return.

That last part was something of an ad lib from Jason and the double meaning did not escape Richard, who suddenly redoubled his efforts. He severely pressed the attack, forcing Jason to take several steps backward and before Graves knew it, his opponent was forcing him ever closer towards a nearby wall.

"Where are your taunting words now? The truth is I've been holding back the entire time, just long enough to know the full measure of your abilities," Richard said even as his feints got closer and closer to Jason, who was obviously on the defensive.

"So, you've been holding back too huh? I'd say it was time for the both of us to stop and show the true measure of our ability," Jason said as he suddenly sidestepped Richard, who lunged at him. Jason knocked him off balance with a solid push of his hand that shoved Richard face first into the wall.

Richard stumbled back for a second, taking time to touch the small amount of blood had started trickling down from one nostril.

"You are going to pay dearly for that!" he stated loudly and charged at Jason and they were at it again. Each one of them fought harder and faster than either of them had previously, because now it was all for real. At first Richard's rage gave him a slight advantage, but as the fight continued it was a ethereal and insubstantial benefit. Jason continually managed to block and counter each of his opponent's attacks, gradually increasing the speed of each of his maneuvers to the point where the strain was starting to show on Richard's face.

Now it was Richard who backed up ever closer to the wall. He was surprised with the speed, skill, and ferocity of his opponent's attack. Before he knew it, he was off-balance again and Jason had managed to cross his sword with Richard's, sending it flying across the tiled floor.

Jason Graves was very much in character, the smug smile once again on his face as he pressed his weapon against Richard's breast. "Submit."

"Never!" Richard protested.

"Submit or die. Those are the only two options," Jason's character explained to his opponent.

Richard was gasping for air and more than a little surprised that Graves had somehow managed to beat him at his own game. But he hesitated just a bit, as he certainly did not like losing to Jason, especially when it meant putting an extra grand into the other man's pocket. However, there wasn't much he could do and the director was motioning to him that the camera was still rolling.

"I submit to your mercy…" Richard said, a bit resigned and accepting that he had indeed lost.

The director shouted, "CUT!" knowing he had captured the best fight scene of his career.

The rest of his time working on the movie was relatively uneventful for Jason. It was the sort of film he had gotten used to as of late. In fact The Rapier was the fourth pirate or swashbuckling movie he had made in the last couple of years, and he was starting to get worried about being typecast. His career hadn't been successful enough to call for him putting up a fight every time Mr. Sturgis, the studio head, sent him a script. He hoped eventually he could get some sort of script approval written into his contract with Constellation Pictures, but as long as they kept paying him to make their movies, he had little reason to complain.

ROBB
ENTERTAINMENT
merchandising
merch.robbent.com

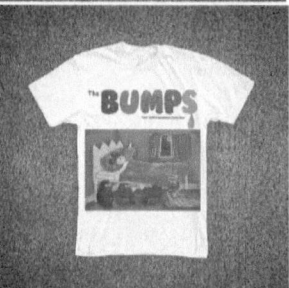

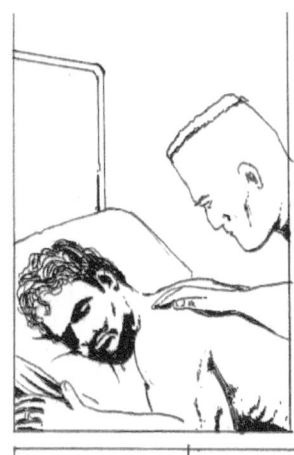

COMING SOON:

The Secret Origin

Of

The Rapier

Chapter Five:

The Debut

of

the Rapier

Time passed and they finished the film and before long the day arrived that Constellation Pictures was readying the premiere of Jason Graves' latest blockbuster. Earlier in the day Charlie drove Jason to Mr. Sturgis' office, for a quick last-minute meeting before the premiere. Jason entered the office. There were several couches and

chairs arranged against two of the walls, as well as some comfortable chairs. The wall behind the large desk covered with various pictures. The stuffed heads of an antelope and wild boar were prominently displayed among the pictures. Studio head Howard Sturgis was sitting at his desk.

"Good day for a premiere, Howard," Jason said.

Sturgis looked up. "Yes it is, glad you could make it before the sun went down. You know I usually try to leave the office by four."

"Oh yeah, my apologies for not getting here earlier, I was a bit indisposed." Jason explained. With the filming over he was sliding back into old habits.

Mr. Sturgis got up and walked around the desk and then sat on it in front of Jason. "Don't sweat it my boy. This new movie of yours will be huge, I tell you," he said enthusiastically.

"It is pretty good isn't it?" Jason said while Mr. Sturgis got up and stepped to his side.

"Pretty good? It's actually crap, but the public loves you, so they'll come and see it," Sturgis plainly stated.

"That bad, huh?" Jason said uncomfortably.

"Of course. You know, it's the pirate swashbuckler stuff you always do."

That hit home. "Yeah, I've been thinking about that lately. Maybe it's time that I made a western, they seem pretty popular." Jason suggested.

"Westerns? Nah, you're not the western type. But that doesn't matter, the premiere is tonight. So I think it would be best if you concentrated on that," Jason's boss said.

"I'll be ready, all dressed up real nice, ready to pose and party." Jason quipped.

"Oh no, no partying for you; you'll be in costume," Mr. Sturgis corrected him.

"What? Not that god-awful thing. You're kidding me!" Jason said with disgust.

"No, not a bit, and I want you to do the scene where you swing down and rescue the girl from a couple of pirates," Howard Sturgis explained to Jason. "The press will simply eat it up. Do you think you can remember your lines?"

"Sure, but... I'll be made a laughing-stock at my own premiere!"

"My premiere and you'll be what you've been for the last couple of years, one of the highest paid actors working at this studio," Sturgis firmly reminded him.

Jason didn't appreciate being talked to that way, but Sturgis was his boss. He knew better than to bite the hand that had made such a point of keeping him so well fed. So in the end he just shrugged and said, "Alright, I'll go along with all of this. I guess with great pay comes great responsibility."

"Good, I'm glad that's settled. There's not much to it, all you need to do is swing down to the first floor, say a few lines, and act like you're punching a couple of stunt men. On your way out, my secretary will give you your wardrobe and accessories for this evening. As always my boy, it's a pleasure working with you," Mr. Sturgis said as he showed Jason to the door.

That night, after a late lunch and a couple of drinks, Jason suited up and Charlie drove him to the premiere. As they pulled onto the street the theater was on Charlie looked in the mirror at his friend.

"Are you okay? You look a bit out of it. You sure you're up to this?"

"I'm fine; a couple of drinks always helps loosen me up before a live performance. You just concentrate on getting me there on time," Jason told his friend.

"Sure thing, I'll drop you off at the rear entrance, and be waiting out front when you're done," Charlie explained as they approached the theater. It wasn't long before Jason was heading inside.

He was somewhat familiar with the people who ran the theater, as it wasn't the first of his movies premiered there. The security guy at the VIP entrance had already been told to watch out for him and more importantly to let him in without being bothered by anyone. Soon Jason was in a service elevator and walking out on the second floor looking down at the festivities on the first level. A theater worker walked up to him.

"You're with the movie people, huh? I heard something about a quick skit performance before the show," he asked uncertainly.

Jason nodded. "Yeah just a little publicity stunt for the movie. See that rope over there that has the banner on it? I'm going to untie it on this end and use it to swing down. Then I'm going to knock around a couple of stunt men before we all take our bows." He said with a certain amount of satisfaction.

"Sounds dangerous!" The kid said.

"Nah, do this sort of thing all the time. Piece of cake," Jason said with a smile.

The two of them heard some sort of commotion going on downstairs, and rushed over to the edge of the balcony to see what was going on. Down below they saw three men with guns pushing people around. One of them grabbed a woman and told her, "Here baby, let me have that necklace you're wearing, looks like it would be worth a mint."

"Take your hands off of my wife!" the husband demanded.

In response the thug hit the man across the brow with his gun and he fell. There were screams and the crowd started to rush away, but the leader of the thieves saw that. He drew his pistol and fired it into the air. "My name is Turk, don't forget it. If you nice rich folks don't want no more trouble, give us what we ask for and we'll be out of your hair real fast."

The man turned toward Jason. "What are we going to do? Those guys don't look like they're fooling around," the young employee asked nervously.

Jason shook his head. "This isn't part of the act. They don't know we're up here. You go call the cops from somewhere safe. I'll see if I can distract them until they get here," he quickly added.

"Alright, I can do that," the boy said and he headed off toward the nearest phone.

Jason looked down and saw two of the thieves were moving through the crowd, looking people over. They didn't look very bright. The other thug called Turk stood away from the crowd and directed his cohorts. He was the leader, the brains of the heist. They didn't know about him. Jason saw his chance to do something truly heroic, something Charlie would warn him not to do but he had to try. He untied the line meant for his dramatic entrance. Holding it to the side, he positioned himself in a pose where everyone can see him.

"Gentlemen! I don't know what dastardly deeds you had planned tonight, but get ready to have them thwarted by The Rapier!"

"Who the hell are you?" Turk said, looking up towards Jason.

"Weren't you listening? I'm The Rapier," Jason repeated.

"Yeah, whatever, looks to me like you're the guy that's about to get himself shot," Turk said as he aimed his pistol at Jason.

Loudly laughing for a moment Jason smiled, "I hope you don't think I'm going to sit here and wait for you to plug me." He hesitated on purpose, for timing was critical. Turk fired and Jason grabbed the line and swung down, slamming into the man and knocking him across the floor, unconscious. The Rapier then leaped to his feet and pulled out his sword, taking a defensive stance.

He addressed the other two thugs. "You boys are going to have to make a quick decision. Maybe you can take me and maybe you can't; doesn't matter because time is running out."

"What do you mean?" one of the other hoods asked. He was still rattled that the costumed fool had taken down the boss.

"Can't you hear those sirens? The cops are already on their way. They were called the moment I saw the three of you come in. I realized you were scum right away," Jason explained.

"He's lying. I don't hear anything. I say we shoot him and get out of here," the other thug stated. They pointed their guns at him, as he rushed the first one. Although they both fired, they narrowly missed him. He ducked and dodged back and forth, acting as his character would have. This got him close enough to stab his rapier into the thug's ankle. The man screamed out in pain and dropped his pistol to the floor. Jason kicked it over to one of the unarmed security guards. He picked it up and leveled it at the man who was still standing. Jason balled up his unoccupied fist and glared at the injured thug.

"If you want to keep all of your teeth, I'd suggest you sit on the ground and wait for the cops. You'll never make it out of here alive. Look at as your friend over there; he's still down for the count. The odds are even more in my favor and time is running out. You sure you can't hear those sirens now?" Jason goaded him. He was still stalling and desperately hoping for more backup.

The entire room had quieted down, as everyone there, including the two thugs, were listening to see if they could hear the sirens that Jason kept talking about. Suddenly a woman exclaimed, "He's right I can hear them! The police are coming!"

The Rapier smiled wickedly. "I'm afraid the game has turned against you. Surrender and you'll live to talk about it. Now drop that gun and kick it over here," he demanded.

The other thug paused for a moment, but then looked around at his two fallen comrades, and it was obvious Jason was right. He could hear the approaching police sirens now. He was alone, in a place surrounded by a crowd of angry people following a costumed hero, and he couldn't shoot all of them. The madman with a sword was facing off with him again. They would send him to the chair if he killed one of these rich people. It was too much for one man, so he did the only reasonable thing: he dropped his gun and surrendered.

Afterward, Jason Graves, who was only an actor playing a part, slumped in relief. When the cops got there, followed quickly by reporters, there was a huge fuss and many witnesses talking all at once. Flashbulbs went off and the headlines the next morning's headlines read "THE RAPIER SAVES THE DAY!"

So, although it was never his intention, that's how the rakish actor

Jason Graves became The Rapier, the world's very first real costumed

adventurer.

Chapter Six:

The

Next

Day

The next day Jason woke before the crack of dawn. He couldn't explain it. For some reason he just seemed full of a strange restless sort of energy. It was similar to what he felt in the early days of his career, back at the beginning when he first started working in film. When he was intrigued by the glamour of it all and the possibilities of what wealth and fame could bring. Then there was the unsteady anticipation of not knowing what could happen in the course of a day.

The life he had lived, growing up in Brooklyn, had taught him the value of competitiveness and firmly establishing his willingness to push himself to whatever lengths were necessary. If a movie needed an actor who could ride a horse, Jason was out on a ranch somewhere learning how to properly ride with several old cowhands who had worked in the early days of film.

It wasn't talent that made Jason Graves the star he was. It was fierce determination. Doing all he could from dawn to sunset. When he failed or made a mistake, he'd just dust himself off and was ready to go again. At night, when they weren't shooting a film, he was living life to the fullest. He was doing shots with some of the heaviest drinkers in Hollywood.

Then there were the women. Women were appreciative of a man living in the Great Depression who was on his way up in the world. He was achieving the American Dream, during the height of the days when a lot of people had given up on such things. At the beginning, there was nearly an endless stream of members of the opposite sex who were all too willing to jump into bed with the fresh young actor with the reputation for pushing himself physically between the sheets just as much as he did in the boxing ring or under the bright lights of film production. Not just the ones that felt good to the touch and were fair to the eyes, but the assertive ones and the ones with professional degrees and proper education. It wasn't long before he found himself tangled up in more than one dangerous tryst with a producer's wife or studio executive's allegedly virtuous daughter.

The thing is, too much of a good thing is a curse. Most of the men in Hollywood had absolutely no interest in pushing themselves, especially physically. Their job was to look good for the cameras and in some cases pretend as if they were physically impressive. Doug had jokingly referred to it as the sad dilemma of being a real man on and off the camera. Like that poor kid Marion who had the bright idea of walking and talking with the swagger and cowboy confidence of one of the better Western stuntmen. Now he had to keep pretending to be something he wasn't everywhere except in the late hours of the night with his wife or one of the many Mexican whores he had developed such a taste for.

Jason had honed the man he was through competition, yet sadly once he reached the pinnacle of fame and fortune as a Hollywood actor, he discovered there wasn't a lot worth competing against. The few men that could out-drink him would be passed out under the table while Jason was busy flirting with their wives. The women who managed to hold his attention for more than a week or so eventually grew bored, or they tired of his inability to commit.

Then to make matters worse, Jason had started getting bored. Bored of too much of a good thing. He just wasn't being challenged any more, and so he focused on keeping his mind occupied with the hedonism which was so freely offered. He didn't mind the bad reputation it brought him. He just didn't like the idea that it had all become so routine. Jason Graves was a man in need of a challenge.

Last night, when he swung down and stopped those thugs, it had his heart pumping and adrenaline flowing like it hadn't in years. It was like getting in the boxing ring with Jack Dempsey after accidentally insulting his mother. It had been years since Jason had felt so alive. After Charlie drove him home and fixed him a nightcap, Jason sat there on the balcony looking at the moon and savoring the sensation. He felt more alive than he had in years. He felt a lot of things, some of which he couldn't even fully comprehend. The Scotch in his glass never tasted better and sitting there looking up at the moon for the first time in his life there was a strange sense of contentment.

Fully energized by the events of the night, he heard Charlie downstairs getting ready for his early morning run. Jason decided to get dressed and join him outside.

"What the heck you doing up at 5:30 in the morning?" Charlie asked looking up at his friend while he finished lacing up his shoes.

"Just thought I would join you. Anything wrong with that?"

"Nah, nothing wrong with it. Just not used to it. Especially when you don't have any work-related reason to be up at this hour, much less joining me for my early morning run around the neighborhood." Charlie said squinting his eyes while scratching behind his left ear.

"Good. Glad we got that settled. Try to keep up." Jason said mockingly suddenly jumping up and darting down the driveway and breaking into a full run towards the sidewalk.

"Jumping Jehoshaphat!" Charlie said under his breath as he chased after his friend.

By the time the two of them made it back to the estate and the sun was prominently in the sky, to both of their surprise there was a crowd of reporters who had driven up and were getting out of their cars headed to the front door.

"Wonder what that's all about?" Charlie asked stopping his friend and pointing the reporters out to Jason.

"Not sure, probably something related to what happened last night. I'll handle them while you go the back way and get started on breakfast."

The two men split up and Jason casually walked up the main driveway. As soon as the reporters realized he was walking up, they surrounded him and started hitting him with a barrage of questions.

"Is it true you risked your life to save all those people last night?"

"Are you and Gloria Reynolds going to tie the knot?"

Jason trying to shield his eyes from the multiple flashbulbs going off said, "What? What are you talking about? Gloria and I are just friends."

"That was a risk you took last night doing what you did, what if your actions had gotten someone hurt?"

Jason replied, "I had no intention of putting anyone's life in danger."

"Is the Rapier a costumed adventurer like in the funny books all the youths are reading today?"

"Boys calm down. You're getting ahead of yourselves. It was just something that happened. I did what I had to do and that's the end of it. Don't make more of it than what it was." Jason said.

Charlie opened the door. "Jason, telephone, I think it's the studio."

"Alright boys, you heard the man. I've got to go." Jason said.

Jason went inside and picked up the phone. "Yes? Speaking. No, I don't know how it happened, Mr. Sturgis. It just did. Yes, I know about all the reporters asking questions. All bunched together waiting on my front doorstep this morning. There were even a couple with them that weren't from the gossip rags."

Jason paused for a moment, switching the phone to his other ear. "I know. Not exactly something I planned. Something that neither of us planned. I don't know what to say. It just happened."

Mr. Sturgis went on and on about the legal ramifications of what happened. Jason ignored much of this, as it mainly had to do with the studio's possible obligations and not his own. In the end, he was just a Good Samaritan who was also an actor wearing the costume from one of their movies. At the end of the conversation, Mr. Sturgis made it clear he wanted Jason and Charlie to meet him in his office. He came up with some sort of plan he wanted to share with them. Jason hung up the phone, told Charlie to put on his driving cap and they headed back to the studio.

Chapter Seven: The Game Continues

"You haven't said a thing since we left the house," Charlie said, flashing a quick look in the mirror at Jason while stopped at a red light.

Jason rubbed his forehead with his fingertips, "This is a mess. Everyone is making such a big deal about it. Making me out to be something we both know I'm not. It's called acting. What I did with those thugs was just what had to be done."

"Yeah, I know. You ain't no hero," Charlie gruffly said as he made a quick maneuver through traffic.

"Exactly," Jason said as he popped open the side panel that released the custom minibar. He then fixed himself a double bourbon since he was less than ten minutes away from his meeting with Mr. Sturgis. When they arrived at the studio, Jason had a slight warm fuzzy feeling. He didn't like going to the studio on days he wasn't working, but he knew he wasn't getting out of this meeting with Sturgis. He thought it would be best to slide into it as casually as he could. His door opened and he stepped out.

"Still don't know why he wants to talk to me too." Charlie said shrugging as they walked toward the front entrance of the main offices.

"No telling. Maybe he's heard you make a mean pot roast and wants the recipe for his wife." Jason joked.

"Hardy har har...very funny. You're a real riot," Charlie fired back with a groan.

They waited for Mr. Sturgis in his office. Jason sat in a chair across from Sturgis' desk and Charlie stood impatiently beside him.

"Graves, if this is another one your hair-brained schemes…! You have no idea how much trouble you could have caused." Mr. Sturgis fumed.

"My scheme? You're the one that set this whole mess up. What did you want me to do just sit there and hope no one got hurt?" Jason asked.

"No, of course not. You know better. What you did was foolish, but a heroic sort of foolish. It could have been a lot worse if you just sat there and did nothing and we both know it." Mr. Sturgis said pausing for a moment to look over at Charlie, "Wouldn't you be more comfortable if you sat down?"

"Huh? Uh...yeah, I guess so." Charlie said slowly, taking a seat to one side of Sturgis' desk.

Jason looked over at his friend. "Better?"

"Yeah."

"You know this could be a great opportunity. Let the newspaper people get a hold of this and run with it. With a little publicity we might have a hit with this new movie of yours." Sturgis explained.

"My movies do well enough. At least they seem to" Jason said not fully understanding where the studio boss was heading with the conversation.

"They do okay. But they could always do better and this could be just what we need to take your career to the next level. Make you a real force within Hollywood. Might even put you in the place where you could have more say-so in the films we put you in. I know you've done more than you fair share of complaining about some of the stinkers we've tried to put you in. This could be your chance to have your pick of upcoming projects." Mr. Sturgis explained.

Jason pondered what was being said. An opportunity to have more control of his career was something he had always wanted. He casually glanced over at his friend Charlie who sat there silently and then back to the studio head. "Fair enough, what would I have to do?"

"Not much. Make a few more public appearances playing the hero they've turned you into until the movie picks up a good solid crowd." Mr. Sturgis said.

"Public appearances? I don't know if I like the sound of that." Jason said, flashing a quick worried look at what that might entail.

"Nothing to worry about. I'll have my secretary figure up the dates and details. You just make sure you're there," Sturgis said, wary of the typical Jason Graves lack of punctuality. Then he turned to Charlie, "You, on the other hand, go on the payroll to make sure laughing boy here stays off the sauce. I'm going to need him at the top of his game."

"But..." Jason protested, not caring much for the turn the conversation had taken.

"Don't worry when all of this is over, I'll pick up your bar tab all across town for an entire month. Do we have a deal?"

"I guess so. Still don't see why you need to put Charlie on the payroll to watch after me." Jason grumbled.

"Cause I feel more comfortable about his chances of keeping you clean and sober if I'm the one paying him, plain and simple. I'll have my secretary call you with more details in the morning." Mr. Sturgis concluded the meeting with a quick firm handshake with both men.

As they headed back outside, Jason glanced at his watch, "Looks like it's about time for my lunch date with Gloria."

"You're right. We better be on our way," Charlie replied as they exited the building.

"You think you could take time out of your busy schedule to drive us over there?" Jason asked sarcastically.

"Geez, what's gotten into you?" Charlie asked his friend as the two of them headed to the car.

Jason stopped a few feet from the car. "I don't know. I guess I was just hoping to put all this Rapier nonsense behind me. Now Sturgis tells me he wants me to start making public appearances? Next thing you know, I'll be opening supermarkets."

Charlie opened the door of the car for his friend. "You're too hard on yourself. You'll make a couple of appearances dressed up as the Rapier and that will be the end of it."

"You're probably right. There's only one problem." Jason said as

Charlie shut the door and got inside the car behind the wheel.

"What's that?" Charlie asked. "I could really use a drink."

Chapter Eight:

Gloria Reynolds

Jason walked up to the front entrance of the restaurant after being dropped off. Charlie used the opportunity to fill up the gas tank and run a few errands. Jason stopped for a moment and turned to the doorman to ask him how long Gloria had been waiting.

"Not long, maybe ten minutes at the most." Floyd the doorman replied.

"You're a good man, Floyd. Do me a favor and run a little interference if the press shows up looking for a quick byline about what happened at the premiere last night," Graves said presenting the doorman with a folded $20.

"Sure thing, Mr. Graves. Be my pleasure," the man said leaning forward to take the money and opening the door for Graves.

It didn't take him long to figure out where Gloria was sitting. Jason and Gloria met early in both of their careers at some random and mainly forgettable cocktail party. As the years passed, he became more appreciative of her independent and somewhat headstrong nature. Making a point of slowly circling around the side of her table, he turned abruptly, feigning surprise that he ran across her once again. "Fancy meeting you here, love. What do I have to do to be able to take you away from all this and make you a proper wife?"

Gloria warmly smiled, both of their gazes upon one another. It spoke volumes about their physical attraction for each other. They were both comfortable with the other and perhaps it was part of the reason they had yet to consummate the relationship, remaining fiercely flirtatious. He was leaning down and she partially stood up to reach out with her hand and carefully cupped the back of his head. She seductively whispered in his ear, "Not much, you'd just have to give up the alcohol, the women, and the excessive gambling."

"How about I give up smoking and promise to only gamble when I'm sober?" Jason said kissing her on the cheek.

"Always with the half-measures and negotiations. Didn't anybody ever bother to teach you the proper way to win a woman's heart is through blind obedience?" Gloria replied, reflexively tapping the top of his hand.

"Uh...nope, can't say anyone ever tried to teach me that one, but then again, I never was one to pay much attention to anyone trying to tell me what to do," Jason said, as he took a seat and his hand slid down, coming to rest slightly below her kneecap.

Gloria leaned back in her chair grabbing his quickly advancing hand and tossing it away. "Feeling a bit forward today, aren't we? It usually isn't until after they bring out the soup I start having to watch out for the old "creeping hands" problem of yours. Any chance this has anything to do with all the papers talking about there being a new hero in town?"

"What do you mean?" Jason asked a bit confused.

"Is it really so bad? You seem so wound up. It's like you're unsure of yourself. You're usually the most confident guy in the room. You were a hero. You stepped up to the plate and defused a dangerous situation with a bit of bravado and gumption. You should be proud of yourself," Gloria said.

"Proud of myself? Humph, I could have gotten myself killed." Jason said looking somewhat indignant.

Gloria grabbed Jason's hand, "I know, I know. Just think what a handsome corpse you would have made."

Jason turned his head and did his best to avoid her gaze, "Somehow I don't find that reassuring." He said to the side even as he rolled his eyes.

Gloria pressed her hand against his, "It's not like that. It's just I haven't seen this much fire in you for quite a while. You're always so damned casual about everything. But this, it's like you're taking the thing as deadly serious as you can. It's a whole other side of you."

Jason looked directly forward and sighed. "I learned a long time ago if someone hits you that hard, you can either dish it right back or fall to the ground and cover your balls."

In that intimate moment between the two of them, not only hearing his words but also witnessing the raw emotion he was expressing about a past he seldom talked about, she was filled with a better understanding of how deeply she allowed herself to care for him. There was a knot in her gut as she smiled flirtatiously, leaning forward seductively, breathing her hot breath against the side of his face, her lips hovering inches away hinting at the potential passion that was just waiting for release.

"You are so right for this, you don't even know. There always was the hint of something more, which is why I even gave you the time of day in the first place. You're not the sort of guy that folds at the first sign of a fight. You never were, as far as I know and sometimes that can make a woman weak in the knees."

Jason shifted so he was looking deeply into her eyes that glistened with emotion. Reaching out with one hand he grabbed the back of her neck pulling the two of them closer as he leaned in and gently proceeded to plant a series of soft kisses that ran from the inside of her shoulder to the outer edge of her earlobe, each one gradually increasing in passionate ferocity. He then whispered in a low seductive growl, "Is that the reason you keep putting up with me?"

Gloria did her best to regain her composure. She had always been physically attracted to Jason. And his charm was undeniable, especially in that particular moment. "Maybe. Maybe that's a part of it, or maybe it's just sometimes when I look into your eyes, I see more than just the blustering braggart you pretend to be. You're a good man in spite of yourself. There's a lot of good you could do."

Jason reflexively winced, "How much good could a guy in tights really do?"

"Better than no one trying at all."

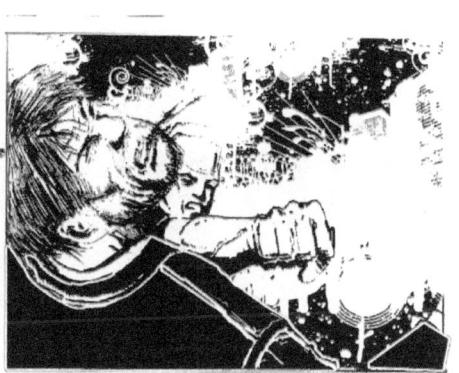

Chapter Nine:

Kiyomitsu

Jason and Gloria enjoyed their meal. She told him about a couple of film projects she was working on. One of them sounded pretty interesting. It was written by a playwright from New York years ago. Quality stuff. Not the usual Hollywood fare, something with bit of a bite to it. Gloria certainly seemed impressed enough. It was so seldom her eyes lit up when talking about a project she was attached to. Then again, it was an issue both of them were used to. Very rarely did an actor working for the studios ever have the right to pick the scripts they worked on. Even more rare for the actresses.

Suddenly, the sounds of a commotion came from the other room. A small group of waiters, accompanied by several Japanese men dressed in business suits entered the room. The waiters immediately rearranged several of the tables in one corner of the room.

"I wonder what that's all about? Everyone's certainly making a big deal about it." Jason asked.

Kiyomitsu walked into the room dressed in a black suit with a vest. He was accompanied by four bodyguards. He was several years older than Jason, slightly graying around the temples. There was a certain regal way that he held himself. This was the sort of man who knew the power of making a dramatic entrance.

"Haven't you heard? He's thes the cousin of the emperor of Japan. He's here for some type of meeting with the top studio executives in Hollywood. From what the papers say, he's here representing his country for a series of meetings with other foreign dignitaries." Gloria explained to him.

Jason looked over at Kiyomitsu and his men and then back at Gloria, "Seems a bit shorter than what you would expect."

"Short? Who cares? He's royalty." Gloria replied back.

"Royalty? He's just the cousin to the emperor of some third-rate country, big deal." Jason said visibly unimpressed.

"Is that a hint of jealousy in your voice?" Gloria said, obviously amused.

"Why would anyone be jealous of him?" Jason asked.

"The money, the power, and the respect he demands? Gloria quipped.

"Oh really? Maybe I need to introduce myself then," Jason said, tossing down his napkin. He got up and headed directly towards Kiyomitsu. Immediately, one of Kiyomitsu's men positioned himself in the way.

Jason sidestepped the bodyguard and was face-to-face with Kiyomitisu. "Nice to meet you. I'm Jason Graves, I'm an actor. You might remember me from one of my films."

The bodyguard looked at Kiyomitsu and he nodded. "I am sorry, you have me at a disadvantage. I have watched very few American movies. My name is Kiyomitsu."

Jason attempted to extend his hand for Kiyomitsu to shake, but the bodyguard got in the way. Jason squared his shoulders toward the man. "You're starting to get annoying," Jason said as he gritted his teeth and balled his hand into a fist.

"Wait!" Kiyomitsu said, as he stood and offered his hand for Jason to shake.

"I think I remember you now. Your picture was in several of the papers this morning. You're the one they are calling a hero."

Jason smiled, firmly shaking the dignitary's hand, "Among other things. It's a pleasure to meet you, your highness."

Kiyomitsu's expression shifted to one of confusion, "Your highness? I am not familiar with your American slang, are you insulting me?"

Jason started to slightly grin at the realization Kiyomitsu had thought he had meant to insult him. "Nah, of course not. Just not sure how to address royalty of your stature. Mind if I take a seat?"

"Yes, you may."Kiyomitsu answered.

Jason proceeded to plop himself down in the chair directly facing Kiyomitsu, "Thanks a bunch. What do you think of California so far?"

Kiyomitsu paused for a moment to glance around the dining area at the various other patrons. "It seems fairly unremarkable so far. The woman you were sitting with when I came in, is she your wife?"

"Gloria? Nah, she's just a friend." Jason said grabbing a glass of water off the table and taking a quick drink as if it was a double Scotch.

"You keep good company for a hero. She is very beautiful." Kiyomitsu remarked.

Jason looked over at Gloria and gave a quick wave of his hand and then turned back to the cousin of the Emperor, "Oh yeah, she's a peach, no doubt. So, what finds you in the good old U. S. of A?

"Just a little official business I need to attend to as an official representative of my country. While I am here I am looking into purchasing a summer home.

"Here let me give you the name of my real estate agent, he's the best in the city." Jason said, pulling out a card and pen. Kiyomitsu's bodyguards visibly tensed up, thinking he might be pulling out some sort of weapon. Kiyomitsu gave them a quick stare and they stop. Jason, not showing that he notices, wrote down his real estate agent's name.

"Thank you, Mr. Graves. It is a gracious act. I appreciate your effort to aid me in my search." Kiyomitsu said as he took the card and handed it to one of his men.

"Who knows? We might even end up neighbors. Anyway, been nice talking to you, but as you can see, I have a beautiful woman waiting for me," Jason said as he got up from the table and returned to Gloria.

Chapter Ten: Playing the Role, Being the Hero

The next day, Jason was in costume and at one of the larger banks in the Los Angeles area. The setup was relatively uninteresting. Several armed thugs, stuntmen hired by the studio, would come into the bank armed to the teeth and announce it was a robbery. Then Jason, dressed as The Rapier, would come sweeping in, overcome the first man with a series of quick punches, then knock out the second one with the hilt of his sword and quickly finish the third with a savage roundhouse right. Things went fairly well and he was actually surprised that judging by the look on their faces some of the customers didn't immediately recognize it was all for show. After he was done and the police and press had left, he was more than ready to call it a day as he slumped back into the car and started to remove his mask.

"That wasn't so bad, boss. I kinda like the idea of you playing The Rapier for the crowds. Good way to get the adrenaline pumping," Charlie said as he eased the car and into the traffic of the day.

"Nope, it didn't go as bad as I thought it would. The main thing is it only took a couple of hours out of my day. Anyway, since I can't drink, I was thinking that we could drop by the tennis club and I could play a couple of rounds," Jason said.

Suddenly there was the sound of gunfire. Two men shot at a car sitting at a stoplight. Before Jason or Charlie could react, the two men opened the passenger door of the car and pulled out a young woman, kicking and screaming and clutching a leather satchel tightly in her hand. Jason was out of the car and pouncing on one of the men, knocking him to the street. The two of them rolled around exchanging punches. The other gunman found himself quickly overcome by several solid punches thrown by Charlie. Each of Charlie's punches knocked the man further and further back until he fell across the car and to the ground.

"What is this all about?" Jason asked as he managed to get on top of the guy and grab his wrist twisting it savagely and knocking the spare gun out of his hand.

"None of your damned business!" was all the man managed to say before Jason knocked a couple of his teeth loose with some solid rights.

It turned out the woman worked for the Los Angeles museum and had been in the process of transferring various items from a local private collection that had recently been donated in its entirety to the museum. The two men must have known this and decided to attack her car before she made it back to the museum. Jason decided it would probably be best for him and Charlie to transport her there with a police escort. Once they arrived the director of the museum thanked them for stopping the robbery in progress and expressed concern there would be another attempt that night when the items would be on display for the first time. Jason suggested he make an appearance as The Rapier to help keep out the riff-raff. The museum director agreed that him being there might make a difference plus it would generate much needed additional publicity for the museum.

Chapter Eleven: Night at the Museum

Jason stood decked out in his Rapier costume at the Museum gala with Charlie at his side. The room was full of evening gowns and wealthy donors in tuxedos.

"I look ridiculous compared to everyone else," Jason admitted.

"I know exactly what you mean, boss. Maybe I should have worn a tux."

The director of the museum walked up to the both of them. "Mr. Graves, I just want to thank the both of you for the added security."

"Glad we could help out, although I doubt we'll be neeeed with all the extra policemen here."

"Probably not, but you being here makes the investors feel better about the whole thing. After all who would be foolish enough to try to rob this place with the Rapier protecting it," the man said with a quick chuckle.

"Boss?" Charlie said.

"What, Charlie?"

His friend motioned over to the staircase where Gloria was making her entrance. She as always was stunning and radiated the sort of raw sexuality only confidence could bring. He had not expected her to show up at the gala but now that she was there, he couldn't keep his eye's off her. She was his glorious distraction.

By the time Gloria made it to the bottom of the stairs he had managed to catch her eye. They both smiled and she walked over to where he was standing next to his driver. "Fancy meeting you here. I must admit, that outfit doesn't leave much to the imagination."

"It's not so bad," Jason replied.

Gloria's eyes shifted briefly downward. "Not from where I am standing," she said smiling.

Jason smiled back and reached for her slipping one arm around her waist. "Nice dress, it brings out your eyes. Makes me want to sweep you off your feet. Did I mention you look amazing. Can't say I was expecting you but I am always appreciative of the company," Jason said as they embraced. He planted a slow seductive kiss on her neckline and whispered in her ear, "Seriously Gloria, what are you doing her?"

"The lovely lady is with me. Spend even the smallest moment with her and you will quickly realize she is the finest treasure in this entire building," Kiyomitsu said as her pulled Gloria away from Jason and gently kissed the back of her hand. "There are a couple of people I wanted you to meet." Kiyomitsu escorted Gloria to another crowded part of the room.

"You okay?" Charlie Gunn asked.

Before Jason can respond the sound of gunfire and screams erupts in the room next to them. Jason hides behind a giant clay statue of a Chinese warrior and Charlie runs to the side of the entrance way. Five men wearing black robes and their faces hidden storm into the room. As the last one enters, Charlie trips him and as he falls hard on the tiled floor, Jason gets between the wall and the statue and pushes it on top of one of the other men, pinning him to the ground.

"We don't want any trouble. Just give us what we want. We're looking for an old jade necklace, "The Claw of the Dragon. We know the museum recently acquired it from an estate donation that included Japanese antiquities."

"I don't give a damn," Charlie said firing several shots into two of the men.

Jason made good use of the distraction, quickly closing the distance to a third thug, knocking the man unconscious with a devastating strike to the side of his head. "Something tells me a certain armed robbery is about to get thwarted," Jason said striking a dramatic pose as he rubbed his chin and gave a wicked smile.

As expected, Jason had drawn the fire of the other two men. It was a dangerous maneuver but he had to get their full attention otherwise they might turn their attacks on someone in the crowd which was the last thing he wanted.

Charlie finished reloading his revolver but before he could fire it one of those Japanese throwing stars struck his hand, knocking the gun to the floor. As he bent down to pick it back up with his other hand, the man's compatriot delivered swift kick to the back of Charlie's legs that brought the big man to the ground.

Jason tackled the man before he could take full advantage of Charlie's prone position. The two men traded blows and they rolled on the ground but eventually Jason managed to get the man in a headlock and it is wasn't long until his opponent had passed out. Now sporting an improvised bandage for his hand, Charlie helped his friend back up on his feet.

"Damn you! You forced my hand. Now give me what I want or the girl dies." The leader of the gang hand one hand wrapped around Gloria's waist and the other held a knife that was leveled at her throat.

"You're right. We have no choice. We'll get you the damned necklace. Just promise me you won't hurt her," Jason said, he could tell even with with a knife at her throat that she trusted him. Trusted that he would find a way to save her. That he could save her. He took a couple of steps towards the assailant and motioned towards the museum director. "You know what he wants. Get him the damn necklace."

"Just like the man said. Get me the damned necklace," The man laughed.

Paying too much attention to the Rapier, the man did not notice

Kiyomitsu so close to his side. But it was too late. The Japanese royal

struck out with the side of his hand into the man's side connecting hard

with his kidney. Kiyomitsu other hand grabbing the man's hand on the

hilt of his blade. The two men fought over the weapon a conflict which

ended with the knife deep in the gut of the thug.

Eventually, the detectives arrived and sorted everything out as best as

they could. By the time they were done it was closing on midnight and

Gloria asked Jason to spend the night at her house. It was everything

he had ever hoped it would be. Although few words were said, neither

could deny the intense attraction they had for each other. It was the

bliss of consummated true love and something both had wanted for

years. Then for a brief time the luxury of sleep with the woman he

loved. But it was only a temporary respite before the men in Japanese

armor attacked Gloria's home and abducted her.

The End.

ROBB
ENTERTAINMENT
merchandising
merch.robbent.com

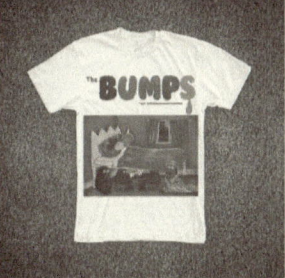

www.ingramcontent.com/pod-product-compliance
Lightning Source LLC
Chambersburg PA
CBHW022019170626

46808CB00003B/981